# Monkey and Elephant Get Better

# Monkey and Elephant Get Better

Carole Lexa Schaefer

illustrated by Galia Bernstein

CANDLEWICK PRESS

To Waldo, my best friend, always and forever
C. L. S.

To Koushirou
G. B.

First edition 2013

Library of Congress Catalog Card Number 2012942656

ISBN 978-0-7636-4841-1

12 13 14 15 16 17 SCP 10 9 8 7 6 5 4 3 2 1

Printed in Humen, Dongguan, China

This book was typeset in Triplex.
The illustrations were created digitally.

Candlewick Press
99 Dover Street
Somerville, Massachusetts 02144

visit us at www.candlewick.com

# Contents

## Chapter One
# DO NOT COPY ME

"I like morning time," said Monkey, dancing in a circle.

"I like morning time," said Elephant, dancing in a circle.

"I like shiny rocks," said Monkey, lifting one.

"I like shiny rocks," said Elephant, lifting one.

"I like to hear my own voice,"
said Monkey. "TAH. TAH. TAH."

"I like to hear my own voice,"
said Elephant. "TAH. TAH. TAH."

"Elephant," said Monkey, "you are copying me."

"Am I?" said Elephant.

"Yes," said Monkey. "I do not like it."

"Why?" said Elephant, swinging his trunk.

"Because you are you and I am me," said Monkey. "We are not just the same."

"Oh," said Elephant. "If you say so."

"I do," said Monkey. "So please—do not copy me. Okay?"

"Um," said Elephant. He shivered a little under the morning sun. "I guess so."

"*Achoo,*" Monkey sneezed.

9

"Achoo," sneezed Elephant.
"ACHOO! ACHOO!"

"Elephant, are you *still* copying me?" said Monkey.

"No," said Elephant. He shivered again. "I don't feel so good."

"Uh-oh," said Monkey.

## Chapter Two
# TAKING CARE OF ELEPHANT

Monkey walked around Elephant as slowly as she could.

"Elephant, you are sick," she said. "I will help you get better."

"Ohh," sighed Elephant. "Thanks."

Monkey brought Elephant some soft hay to rest on and some fresh water to drink.

Elephant dipped the hay into the water and *splapped* it on his head.

"Ahh, that feels good," said Elephant.

Monkey looked surprised.

"Elephant," said Monkey, "you must stay cool in the shade."

"No," said Elephant. "I must stay warm under the sun."

"Hmm," said Monkey. She scratched one pink ear.

"Now," said Monkey, "I will do some tah-dah! juggling to cheer you up."

And she juggled:

one rock

with two hands,

two rocks

with one hand,

three rocks

with four hands — "Tah-dah!"

23

Elephant laughed and laughed.
"What fun! I could *never* copy
that," he said. "I do feel better."

"Good," said Monkey. Then she sneezed: *"Achoo, achoo, ACHOO!"*

"Oh, dear," said Elephant.

❧❧❦❧❧

## Chapter Three
# TAKING CARE OF MONKEY

Elephant swung his trunk slowly—
*whish, whish.* "Monkey, now *you*
are sick," he said. "I'll help you get
better."

Monkey blew her nose — *wonk!*
"Thanks," she said.

Elephant brought some fresh water and some soft hay for her to *splap* on her head.

"Ahh," said Monkey.

She sipped the water. She took a rest on the hay.

Elephant looked surprised.

"Monkey," said Elephant, "you must warm up under the sun."

"No," said Monkey. "I am already too warm."

"Oh," said Elephant. He fanned her with his big ears.

"Now," said Elephant, "I will play my elephant-trunk trumpet for you."

He played loud—

*WAH, WAH, WAH.*

He played soft —

wah, wah, wah.

He played loud and soft together —

WAH wah,

WAH wah,

WAH wah.

Monkey clapped and clapped.
"I feel *much* better now," she said.
"Only *you* can trumpet like that."

"Thanks," said Elephant. "We're both pretty good at what we do."

"Do you know how we could get even better?" said Monkey.

"How?" said Elephant.

"Practice," said Monkey. She juggled two shiny rocks. "So, how about I juggle while you trumpet?"

"'Cause you are you and I am me," said Elephant. "Let's do it!"

41

And,
*WAH, wah, WAH,*
they did.